Wait Until Spring

by
Anne Schraff

Perfection Learning® Corporation
Logan, Iowa 51546

Editor: Pegi Bevins
Cover Illustration: Doug Knutson
Cover Design: Deborah Lea Bell
Michael A. Aspengren

©2000 Perfection Learning® Corporation.
All rights reserved. No part of this book may be
used or reproduced in any manner whatsoever
without written permission from the publisher.

For information, contact
Perfection Learning® Corporation
1000 North Second Avenue, P.O. Box 500
Logan, Iowa 51546-0500.
Tel: 1-800-831-4190 • Fax: 1-712-644-2392
Paperback ISBN 0-7891-5139-1
Cover Craft® ISBN 0-7807-9282-3
Printed in the U.S.A.
4 5 6 7 8 9 10 PP 08 07 06 05 04 03

1 Amelia Kintz let out a terrified scream. She flailed her arms wildly, hitting her younger sister who slept in the same bed.

Thirteen-year-old Tillie jumped. " 'Melia! You're having another nightmare! Wake up!" she shouted.

At 16, Amelia was the oldest of the four Kintz children. Even so, the ocean voyage from Germany had frightened her more than the others. Tillie, little Pauline, and the baby, Joseph, had seemed more excited about the trip than frightened.

Now the family was finally settled in Ohio. But Amelia kept reliving the awful voyage in her dreams. Most of all, she kept remembering the November 1855 storm and the chaos among the passengers. The frantic mothers in search of their children. The strong men struggling against ropes and waves. The screams. The prayers.

Amelia looked at Tillie with wild eyes. "Tillie, the barrels! Do you remember how the barrels rolled around on deck and almost crushed us?" she cried.

"Yes, yes, but all that's past now," Tillie said sternly. She almost acted as if she were the older sister. "We're here and we're safe, Amelia. Now go back to sleep."

Amelia sat up in bed. Shivering, she clutched the blanket against her chest. She recalled how rolling black clouds had filled the sky, as if the end of the world were at hand. She could almost feel the torrents of rain that swept the deck that day. And in her mind, she could hear the ship as it moaned and groaned like a dying beast in the wild sea.

Amelia needed to talk about the horror of the voyage. She needed to talk about the people who had died and whose bodies were thrown overboard. And especially, she needed to talk about 20-year-old Billy Krueger.

"I shall never forget poor Billy," she continued even though Tillie had lain down again and turned her back to her. "We all had ship fever. But Billy went stark-raving mad! Do you remember?"

Billy had been so handsome, with golden blond hair and the bluest eyes Amelia had ever seen. He was pleasant too. He had spoken to her several times at the start of the voyage. Once he had even complimented her on being a fine young woman.

" 'Melia, go to sleep!" Tillie scolded. "There is nothing we can do about any of that now. You know what Mother says. 'Enough for the day are the troubles therein.' "

Amelia lay back on her bed with a heavy sigh. She remembered how Billy Krueger had roamed the deck that last day, wild-eyed and agitated. He insisted that he was a Prussian general making battle plans for some great war. Then, before any of the other passengers knew what was happening, he plunged into the sea and vanished from their sight.

Poor Billy, Amelia thought again, hot tears slipping from her eyes. But she was not weeping just for Billy Krueger. She was weeping for the life she had left behind too. The Kintz home in Bavaria had been so comfortable, so nice. But war and turmoil had taken over Germany. And Amelia's parents had decided that it was time to leave the old country and come to America.

Now Amelia and her family lived in a one-room shanty with a dirt floor. It was cold and filthy. Amelia missed her old home in Germany. She missed her friends. Her cousins. Her grandmother and grandfather. Amelia missed *everything* about the old country.

What will become of us? Amelia worried, drawing the blanket closer. Jacob Kintz had been a shoemaker in Germany. But would her father's skills be good enough for America? she wondered. The family had saved enough money to last for one more month if they were very frugal. But what then? What if her father couldn't find work? How would they buy coffee, sugar, and potatoes? How would they get milk for little Joseph?

Last night her father had talked to Amelia about their situation. "You are a strong, intelligent young woman, Amelia," he had said. "Tomorrow we shall both set out to find work."

That scared Amelia most of all. She trembled at the very thought of trying to please an employer. She knew how to sew, but would she be good enough to sew for Americans? What if she had to work for some cruel tailor who cursed her for every misplaced thread?

Amelia lay back down on the bed. She closed her eyes and tried to sleep. But between the frightful voyage of the past and the uncertainly of the future, she spent a very restless night.

In the morning the family gathered around the wooden table Jacob Kintz had made when they first arrived. They ate johnnycake made with cornmeal and water. If it had been made with milk, it would have tasted much better, Amelia thought. Not even the bit of molasses was much help in swallowing the grainy bread. But it was warm and filling. And it would have to suffice on this cold March morning.

"Did you wash your face, 'Melia?" her father asked. "If we are to find work, we must put on our best faces, *ja?*"

Amelia nodded glumly. She wasn't at all eager to look for work.

"I wish I were older," Tillie whined. "I would rather go to work than sit in a schoolroom."

"You must go to school, Tillie. You must work hard and learn well. Especially English," Mrs. Kintz said. She was trying to feed a squirming Joseph some oatmeal with a few drops of milk. Milk was so dear that there was only enough for Joseph. And there was not even very much for him.

"I am good at sewing," Tillie insisted. "I could earn money too. And then we'd have so much more."

Amelia envied her little sister. She was so brave, so eager to take on new challenges. Amelia silently scolded herself. Why was she so timid, so fearful? Her grandmother had often described her as "a little rabbit frozen with fear." That's how Amelia felt right now.

"Well," Mr. Kintz sighed as he got up from the bench, "off we go, Amelia. Many people are looking for work. But we shall be the early birds getting the worms, *ja?*"

Amelia followed her father across a little bridge, then down the dirt path that led to the roadway. Small shanties dotted the settlement. They provided shelter for the German families who had settled there. Mr. Dietrich, who ran the general store, owned over 100 acres. He sold the land cheaply to new immigrants because he wanted customers for his store.

Amelia glanced at the rickety shanty of each neighbor as they passed. Mr. Gerhardt was an out-of-work glassblower. Mr. Miller, the blacksmith who lived next door, had been lucky enough to find work. But Mr. Kirschner, the laborer in the next shanty, had found none.

Then Amelia and her father passed the Eulmann dwelling. Mr. Eulmann was a talented cabinetmaker. His poor young wife had consumption, a terrible lung disease. Amelia could sometimes hear her coughing all the way down the street.

Another neighbor hailed Amelia's father as they passed. "Jacob!" he called. "I have heard of a shoemaker in town who needs a helper. Mr. Rieb is a demanding man. But if you do good work, it should be a chance for you."

"Thank you!" Mr. Kintz shouted. He smiled at Amelia and they hurried their steps toward town where Mr. Rieb ran his cobbler business. The Rieb family had arrived from Germany several years before. Mr. Rieb made and repaired shoes from the front room of his tidy frame house. Many families who had arrived in America earlier were prosperous now. They lived in neat frame and brick homes with fine furniture. And they could afford nice leather shoes.

"Someday we shall live like those people. We'll have a good, warm house and furniture to be proud of," Amelia's father said.

Mr. Rieb answered the knock at the door. He let Amelia and her father inside. Mr. Kintz removed his hat and began the introductions. "I am Jacob Kintz, and this is my daughter, Amelia," he said in a nervous voice. "She is a seamstress, and I am a shoemaker. We are both seeking work. A neighbor told me you have need of a helper."

Mr. Kintz's voice shook as he spoke. Amelia noticed that he gripped his hat to steady his trembling hands.

Mr. Rieb was a thin, short man with a face as pale as cream. He had dull blond hair and a drooping mustache that stuck

WAIT UNTIL SPRING

to his face like two wet leaves. "Are you a good worker, Kintz?" he asked. Amelia thought she detected doubt in his voice.

"Very good," Mr. Kintz answered, trembling even more. Poor Father, Amelia thought. He was almost 40 years old. But still he stood like a frightened schoolboy, quaking in his boots. And I am just like him, Amelia realized sadly. I, too, will probably always be frightened of new things.

Still, even though her father trembled, he was trying to find work. That showed courage, didn't it? Amelia asked herself. Mr. Kintz had been afraid to leave Germany and come to America. But he came anyway. Maybe that was it, Amelia reflected. One could not stop feeling frightened. But one could rise above the fear to do what needed to be done.

"Come," Mr. Rieb said. "Show me your work."

He led them into a large room filled with cobblers' tools. Amelia inspected all the familiar items. Wooden forms of different-sized feet over which leather would be stretched. Hammers and pointy awls to pierce holes in the leather for laces.

Mr. Kintz picked up a tool and began to work. As Amelia watched, her heart ached for him. Mr. Rieb's alert little eyes followed every movement of her father's skilled hands as he tried to prove his competency as a shoemaker.

After what seemed like a long while, Mr. Rieb said, "You will do for a helper, Kintz. You may start at once. I will pay you five dollars a week."

"Five dollars a week!" Amelia's father cried. His face plainly showed his disappointment in the paltry wage. Earlier he had told Amelia that good shoemakers were making seven dollars or more in America.

Mr. Rieb sneered and said, "If that is not enough for you, then be gone! There are many men, better than you, who would be glad to get five dollars a week."

"*Ja, ja,*" Mr. Kintz added quickly. "I will take it."

Amelia could hardly bear to look at her father's dejected face. She reached out to touch his hand and smiled encouragingly.

"You have found work, Father!" she said. "I will go home and tell Mother right away."

Amelia wanted to return home now and put off the dreaded task of finding a job for herself.

"*Nein*," her father said. "You must try to find work too, 'Melia. The day is young. Ask at the tailor shops. Go to the dry goods store. They might know where a seamstress is needed."

Amelia sighed as she turned to leave her father. She stepped out of the Rieb house and shivered when the brisk March wind hit her. A light snow had fallen, but already it was dirty and gray from chimney soot.

As she walked, Amelia remembered the family farm in Bavaria. The sweet little house where they had lived. The pretty doilies on the arms of the chairs. They had sold it all to come to America. She shook her head. Now they worked like dogs and lived like pigs, she mused.

I wish we had not come here, Amelia thought as she approached a tailor shop. I wish we had stayed in Germany, in spite of the revolutions and unrest.

Inside the shop, the tailor told Amelia he did not need anyone. Amelia felt relieved and started for home. She was anxious to tell her mother that she had tried but had failed to find work. But then she passed the dry goods store. Her father had told her to stop there, and she could not disobey him.

Amelia stepped timidly into the store. Standing behind the counter was a woman with thick brown braids wrapped around her head. Multicolored bolts of cloth were piled everywhere. Under her thin shawl, Amelia felt cold and small as she stood before the woman. She yearned to go home and sit by the stove. But in a small voice, Amelia began, "I am a seamstress and . . ."

"Speak up, child," the woman demanded. "Don't stand there mewling like a sick lamb."

"I am seeking work as a seamstress," Amelia said, this time more assertively.

The woman tilted her head to examine Amelia. "I have need of a girl to help me in the store. And there would be a bit of sewing too. Are you strong enough to lift the bolts down for the customers?" she asked. Before Amelia could answer, the woman continued, "You must be able to stand on your feet for long hours without whining and complaining. I cannot abide that. I will give you four dollars a week," she finished tersely.

Amelia's heart sank. The woman seemed so unkind. Plus, it would be hard work lifting the heavy bolts of cloth from the high shelves. And four dollars a week was so little! Surely someone would hire her for more money.

"Well, what do you say?" the woman asked impatiently. "Or has the cat got your tongue?"

"I had wished for a job as a seamstress," Amelia replied simply.

" 'If wishes were fishes, beggars would eat,' " the woman quoted an old proverb scornfully.

Just then a young man appeared. He had blond hair and bushy eyebrows. And he looked to be about 18. He resembled Billy Krueger, Amelia thought, although he was not quite as handsome.

The young man's gaze fixed on Amelia

and lingered there. A tiny smile danced on the edge of his lips. Amelia could tell at once that he liked her.

"Have you hired this girl to work for you, Mother?" he asked the woman with the braids. "She looks to be a fine choice!"

"This girl has not yet decided if the job is good enough for her," the woman scoffed.

"Come and work here," the young man said warmly. "I am Herman Wallace, and I can tell you that you will like working for my mother. She is not as stern as she sounds. If you work here, you can buy cloth cheaper than other people. And you can make pretty dresses for yourself—to match your eyes."

Amelia was taken aback by his words. Her heart quickened. In just a few seconds, this young man had charmed her, she realized. He seemed so kind, so genuinely interested in her.

She dropped her eyes as she felt her cheeks go warm. "Yes, I will work for you, Mrs. Wallace," she said.

For the first time since coming to America, Amelia had met a stranger who had gone right to her heart.

2

"Mrs. Wallace is not too pleasant, but her son is very kind," Amelia explained to her parents that evening. The family was sitting together at the table. They were eating sauerkraut and hard little dumplings made from flour and water. Pork would have tasted delicious with the sauerkraut. But they could not afford it now.

"His name is Herman," Amelia continued. "He has already promised to build me a ladder so it will be easier to go up and down with the bolts of cloth."

Mrs. Kintz beamed. "Our daughter will be bringing home four dollars a week!" she said to Mr. Kintz. "With the money the two of you make, we can buy milk, cheese, and meat. Maybe even a horse and wagon too!"

"I would like a *milch* cow," Tillie said. "The Eulmanns have a fine cow. They have enough milk, cream, and cheese for themselves, and they even have some to sell."

"Mrs. Eulmann has consumption," her mother said sadly. "That is why they bought the cow. So she has fresh milk to drink. So she gets stronger."

"She will get well, won't she?" Amelia questioned. Mrs. Eulmann was such a beautiful woman. She had great dark eyes and hair the color of honey.

Mr. Kintz looked at his daughter and answered grimly, "Maybe she will, and maybe she won't." Amelia looked down at her plate and said no more.

For a long while Amelia's father was quiet as he ate his sauerkraut and bland dumplings. Finally he said slowly, "Mr. Rieb is a very hard man. He is not easily satisfied. He tormented me with threats all day long. 'You call this good work, Kintz?' he said. 'You tell me why I ought not kick you out into the street.'"

His wife touched his arm. "Oh Jacob . . . it will get better. Mr. Rieb will soon recognize your skills. Then he will be kinder. You will see."

Amelia worried that her father might lose his job. Her four dollars a week would not be enough for the family. And what of her own job? If her work didn't please Mrs. Wallace, what then?

That night Amelia's new worries chased away any nightmares about the ocean voyage. But in the morning she ate the dry johnnycake with molasses and then set off with her father. The day was new. And although she was scared, she was also proud. She would be paid for her work. And that made her feel important in a way she'd never felt before.

The air was very cold as father and daughter walked toward town. But the sun was beginning to rise, with the promise of a blue and cloudless sky to come.

"I would like a shoemaking business of my own," Mr. Kintz confided in Amelia. "It is hard to be under the thumb of another man."

"Lottie says it's easy to get ahead in America," Amelia said. Lottie Miller was the daughter of the blacksmith who lived near Amelia's family. "I don't believe it though. I think it must be difficult. But Lottie told me her father will soon have his own smithy. And then they'll have money."

When they reached Mr. Rieb's shop, Mr. Kintz gently grasped Amelia's shoulders. He looked seriously into her eyes and said,

"Work hard today, *liebkin*. Do an honest day's work. But watch yourself around Herman Wallace. If young men grow too friendly, it may be because they are not honorable. As you know, my brother Peter took his wife and children to New York. Now his daughters are ruined."

"Katrina and Lizzie? My cousins? Ruined?" Amelia asked in shock. She had heard nothing of this before. She was horrified.

"*Ja,*" her father said, "they are bad now. The city has ruined them. So you be on watch, Amelia." Then he turned and vanished into the cobbler's shop.

Amelia slowly walked toward the dry goods store, thinking about her father's warning. Her cousins had brought shame upon their family. Silently Amelia swore that she would never allow herself to do that.

Mrs. Wallace was waiting impatiently for her when she reached the store. "So at last you are here! You must cut some of the dark red bolt. Mrs. Dietrich is coming by to pick it up. You know how to measure three yards, don't you?"

"Oh yes," said Amelia. She quickly cut the three yards and placed them on the counter for Mrs. Dietrich.

All morning Amelia worked hard, and by midday her back ached. Herman had not yet built the ladder for her. So she had to climb on a chair and stretch to get the heavy bolts piled on the high shelves.

Just before the store closed, Herman appeared with the ladder. It was a fine, firm ladder. "This will be so much better, Miss Kintz," he said.

Amelia thought it sounded strange to be called "Miss Kintz," as if she were a grown-up lady. She giggled to herself at the sound of it.

When it was time to leave, Herman offered to walk Amelia to her house. "Rough men sometimes stand on the corners and act very uncivil," Herman explained. "Surely a pretty girl like you would attract their attention."

For the second time, Herman Wallace caused Amelia to blush. This time he had told her she was pretty. On the voyage from Germany, Billy Krueger had paid her a compliment too. But whenever Amelia peered into the looking glass to comb her hair, she thought she was as plain as mud. She could see nothing pretty about her common features.

Herman guided her out the door. As they began walking, Amelia asked, "Have you lived in America a very long time, Mr. Wallace?"

"Yes," he answered. "I was five when we left the old country. So I don't remember much about it. Father bought the dry goods store here. Then he suffered heart failure and died. But he left Mother and my sister and me with sufficient money."

It suddenly occurred to Amelia that soon they would arrive at the horrid shantytown where she lived. Then Herman would see the awful squalor of the settlement. She was nearly overcome with shame at what he would think.

"We have just come to America," she explained, trying to soften the shock. "For now, we must make do. But we are getting more prosperous every day. And soon we shall have a nice home."

Herman placed his hand protectively on

Amelia's back as a horse and wagon rattled by, spewing mud. A thrill ran through her body at his gentle touch. "You are very kind, Mr. Wallace," she said.

He chuckled and then reached into his pocket. "I have something for you," he said. "Do you know about *Godey's Lady's Book?*"

"No," Amelia admitted. She stared at the magazine in his hand.

"My sister likes this book very much," Herman said. "But it is too old for her. She is just 12, and she enjoys playing the little lady. This magazine tells about all the new dress styles and how to decorate a room. A young lady like you should enjoy it."

"Thank you very much," Amelia said as she took the book. She glanced swiftly through the pages. She saw a few recipes and patterns that could be useful. But in general, the magazine represented a way of life far different from the one the Kintz family lived. Amelia worried about how Herman would react when he saw where she lived.

"You have brought me far enough," Amelia said promptly. "I shall go the rest of the way myself."

"No, no," Herman insisted. "Look up ahead at those run-down houses. Who knows what kind of people live there. You might be in danger from them."

Amelia felt the blood stop in her veins. She watched a small group of grimy boys pelting one another with clods of frozen earth. A drunken man staggered down the hill. He clung to trees and fence posts in an effort to keep his balance. Amelia cringed in shame.

Her feet slowed and then stopped moving altogether. She tried to explain the Kintzes' situation. "You see," she said in a halting voice, "my family sold everything we had in Bavaria to come here to America." She wrung her hands and continued, "We had to buy one of the cheap lots in the settlement..."

Amelia's voice faltered as she gazed toward the settlement. In the distance, she could see her mother and Pauline outside. They were hanging wash on the line strung from their shanty to a stark tree.

Herman stared at her blankly. Suddenly he grasped her meaning. "Oh, I see," he said, the warmth now gone from his voice. "You live down there . . . well then, good night, Miss Kintz."

As he turned to leave her, his condescension was clear. And Amelia's heart ached.

She hurried the rest of the way alone. Her cheeks burned with shame and anger. He will not give me compliments again, or even give me a second look, she thought. And who could blame him? He wasted *Godey's Lady's Book* on a girl who lives in a pigsty! Amelia desperately wished she could have told him about the house in Bavaria. The good furniture. The little flower garden. The potted plants in the windows. But he was gone, and it was too late.

"Amelia!" Lottie Miller spotted her and ran to her side. "How is your work at the dry goods store?"

"It's very hard," Amelia said crossly. "My back hurts."

"Who was that handsome man who was walking with you?" Lottie asked curiously.

"He's the son of the woman I work for," Amelia answered.

"He seemed to like you," Lottie said with a knowing wink.

"Oh, Lottie!" Amelia cried. "He is a fine young man who lives in a pleasant house. Now he knows that I live in this filthy settlement. He knows the miserable way we live. How we go to the slaughterhouse and beg bones for dogs we do not own, so our families may eat! That our little brothers and sisters have clothing made from flour sacks. He thinks we are barbarians—and we are. Why should he like me?" Amelia was so hurt and angry that she began to cry.

" 'Melia, don't be foolish," Lottie scolded gently. "We are as good as those who live in town. But we are only beginning. Just wait. I will get good clothes, and so will you. I will get a silk frock when Father has his own smithy. We will get pretty straw bonnets for the summer too. Soon we will have fine homes and nice furniture. And pretty flowers in the windows. We cannot be downhearted."

Amelia fell into Lottie's arms and cried out all her tears. When she wiped her eyes, she drew back with a wistful smile. "You're right, Lottie," she said. "I don't know what came over me. I have a foolish heart. I see a handsome boy, and I melt like butter on a griddle. It was the same thing with Billy Krueger on the voyage. I scarcely knew him. Yet I grieved his death as if he were my sweetheart!"

Arm in arm, the girls walked toward their shanties. They heard Mrs. Eulmann racked by another coughing spell as they passed her house.

"She is dying," Lottie whispered sadly. "Father says so."

"No, just wait until spring," Amelia protested. "She will be better when the cold weather is over and the days are warm again."

"She is only 22 and has two children already," Lottie reflected. "A two-year-old and a three-year-old. Poor Mr. Eulmann. He works so hard as a cabinetmaker. But now he is afraid to leave her side and go to his shop. He brings work home and does as much as he can there. What will become of the children when she dies?"

While they spoke, Moritz Eulmann

stepped out of the door with his children. He was tall and lean, with tousled black hair and a shaggy beard. He had big dark eyes, like smudges of ash. On his arm, he held the little boy, Albert. Three-year-old Minnie clung to his trouser leg timidly.

Amelia noticed that the children's clothing looked worn and dingy. Minnie's tangled braids were in much need of attention, and Albert's nose was running. Mr. Eulmann looked wasted and gaunt. It was as if his wife's illness were destroying him as well. But despite his unkempt appearance, Amelia could see that he was a very handsome man. She thought that he and Mrs. Eulmann must have made a fine couple on their wedding day. But now Mrs. Eulmann was terribly sick. And poor Mr. Eulmann was carrying the weight of the world on his shoulders.

Amelia was struck with pity. She called, "How is your wife, Mr. Eulmann?"

Mr. Eulmann glanced at his children before answering. "You know, Amelia, I think she is a little better today," he said with false confidence.

Amelia knew that the lie Mr. Eulmann

had just told was meant to save his children from any more worry. She felt sorry for the man and his family, but she smiled and said, "I'm so glad."

Then she grasped Lottie's hand. The two friends hurried toward their own shanties at the end of the settlement.

Snowflakes were falling by the time Amelia arrived home. Mrs. Kintz had used a portion of their meager savings to buy food. Now the fragrance of potatoes and pork ribs with sauerkraut filled the tiny house. Tonight they would have a special feast to celebrate the good fortune of employment.

Amelia anticipated the tasty food so much that, for the moment, she forgot everything that had pained and sorrowed her that day.

3

As the Kintz family savored the flavorful food that evening, Mr. Kintz seemed full of optimism. For the first time since the family had arrived in America, Amelia saw his familiar smile and heard his easy laughter.

"Today, old Rieb had his eyes opened," her father reported. "A very good customer came in to have her shoes repaired. When she picked them up, she could not get over the nice job. She said, 'Mr. Rieb, you always do a good job. But this time it is even better!' And old Rieb did not say a word. But he knew I did the repair. He took the compliment as if it were for him. But now he knows he needs me!"

Mrs. Kintz clapped her hands and said, "Ah, Jacob! Good! Good!"

Mr. Kintz smiled even wider and continued. "Just before I left for home, old Rieb came to me and said, 'You are pretty good, Kintz. I think you are worth six dollars a week!' Just think!" Amelia's father exclaimed. "Another four dollars every month!"

"You are worth even more than that," his wife insisted. Then she turned to her daughter. "And how is your work at the store, Amelia?"

"Mrs. Wallace is satisfied with me," Amelia replied. She stared down into her sauerkraut as she spoke.

Mr. Kintz said, "Old Rieb told me the Wallaces do not like anything that is German. Mrs. Wallace is German, but her husband was not. Mr. Wallace thought he was better than the German folk. He used to say that Germans were dirty and lazy!"

"Dirty!" Mrs. Kintz cried as if the insult were directed straight at her. "German homes are the cleanest of any homes!"

Amelia's head jerked up sharply. "Our home is not clean," she said. She was still stinging from the humiliation she felt when Herman saw where they lived. "How can we be clean when our floor is made of dirt?"

"Amelia!" her father scolded. "We are just newcomers to America. We are doing the best we can."

Amelia dropped her head and nodded. She was ashamed of her fiery outburst. She knew her father was right. But Amelia could not help feeling embarrassed about it all. She hated their shabby home. She hated her worn, shapeless dress. She hated her dirty, oversized shoes.

Mr. Kintz patted Amelia's hand gently and said, "Soon we will have enough money to put in a board floor. We will build another room for sleeping. You will see what a difference that will make."

Her father continued his convincing talk. "Miller has a good job at the blacksmith's, and he will build onto his house soon. And when Gerhardt gets a good job, he will build onto his house too. You will see, 'Melia. Nice houses will be standing here soon. There will be gardens and potted plants in the windows. And you'll have new clothes to wear as well. Things will be better in the spring."

Tillie had been eating in silence. But now she piped up, "I just want for us to have a *milch* cow. The Eulmann's cow is so sweet. I would like one just like her."

"I want a cow too!" Pauline squealed. "I will ride her."

Tillie laughed. "No, no. You ride a horse. A cow is for milk."

While the rest of the family laughed and

chattered, Amelia thought about what her father had said. And what she had said to Lottie about Mrs. Eulmann. We all seem to be waiting for spring, she thought. A time of rebirth. A time of hope. But would things *really* be better then? She sighed and hoped with all her heart that they would.

***

When Amelia went to work the next day, Mrs. Wallace was not there. Herman stood behind the counter instead. Amelia entered hesitantly, avoiding his eyes. She expected him to be very distant. But he smiled as he greeted her, and he seemed friendlier than ever. Amelia was perplexed.

"You must try the nice ladder I made for you," he suggested cordially. "A customer will be coming in soon for some of that blue cloth on the shelf. Why don't you use the ladder and get it down now?"

"All right," Amelia replied.

Herman held the ladder firmly for her, and she mounted the sturdy rungs.

Amelia easily lifted the bolt of cloth off the shelf. As she came down the ladder, she felt Herman's hands encircle her waist. "Here, let me steady you, Miss Kintz," he said. "I don't want you to fall."

Amelia was taken aback by his touch. Never had an unfamiliar man put his hands around her waist. She had felt no danger of falling, so his help wasn't truly necessary. But perhaps he was being extra careful with her because he was such a kind and caring young man, she thought.

"Thank you," she said politely when she reached the floor. As she set the bolt of cloth on the counter, she sensed that Herman was close behind her. He placed his hands on her shoulders and gently turned her so she faced his warm smile.

"We are friends, aren't we?" he asked.

"Oh yes," answered Amelia. She was delighted that he thought so. From the very first moment she saw him, she had been thrilled by his attention. But after yesterday she was afraid he would have nothing to do with her.

"Would it be agreeable if I called you

Amelia?" Herman asked. "Since we are friends," he added quickly.

"Yes, I'd like that," Amelia said.

"Then you may call me Herman," he replied.

Amelia nodded. She was filled with joy! Herman still liked her even though he had seen the terrible place where she lived. In fact, it seemed he liked her even better than before. What a wonderful young man he was! He could look beneath the squalor of the settlement. And he could see that she and her family were quality people endeavoring to begin a life in a new land.

"I think you must be a very good carpenter," Amelia said, "because this is a very good ladder."

Herman laughed and replied, "I'm not really a carpenter. My father taught me to work with wood. But I have more important plans for my future. I study at Ohio University, and someday I will become a lawyer."

Amelia was awed. A university student! Herman was a university student, *and* he liked her. Back home in Bavaria, a university professor had once come to visit the Kintz family. He was a very distant cousin. Amelia always considered him a great person. And to think Herman aspired to the law!

"That is wonderful, Herman," she said genuinely.

Herman shoved back a cowlick of blond hair and smiled. "You are wonderful too, Amelia."

Amelia gave a grateful smile and turned quickly back to her work. But her fingers trembled, and her heart pounded with excitement. It was hard to concentrate on the work of measuring and cutting.

When she was finished for the day, she put her shawl around her shoulders and headed out the door. Herman rushed to join her. "Can I walk you home again, Amelia?" he asked.

Amelia hesitated. "Do you want to?" she asked.

"Yes," Herman answered. "I like walking you home. But first let's go down to the edge of the woods and see the crocuses." He pointed across the dirty snow-covered field toward a line of bare trees. "There's still some ice and snow on the ground. But a few crocuses are blooming behind that row of apple trees. I thought you might like to see them."

Grasping Amelia's hand, he led her through the ruts to a tiny, shaded snow bank. Amelia saw a clump of golden crocus blooms peeking from the snow. "Oh! How beautiful!" she exclaimed.

Herman reached out and smoothed Amelia's long hair away from her face. His fingers brushed her neck. "You should have a dress that color, Amelia," he said. "It would make your pretty face even prettier."

"Thank you," Amelia replied, still puzzled at his insistence that she was pretty.

Her mother had once said that every family had one pretty daughter, one vivacious daughter, and one who was good and quiet. Sadly, Amelia always placed herself in that last position. Tillie had the lively personality, and Pauline would be the most beautiful of the three. But now she wondered if perhaps she was lovely and sparkling in her own way.

Otherwise, would this wonderful young man be so taken with her?

"Thank you for showing me the lovely crocuses, Herman," she said. "But now I must be getting home."

"Of course," Herman replied. He led her across the field again and to the edge of the shanty settlement.

"Thank you again, Herman," Amelia said.

"We will see each other at the store tomorrow, eh?" Herman said, taking her hand and squeezing it.

"Yes, tomorrow," Amelia answered. As she turned toward the settlement, she could still feel the warm pressure of his hand. And she couldn't help but smile. She decided to stop at the Millers' house and tell Lottie her exciting news.

"Oh, Lottie," Amelia told her friend. "I told you about Herman, the son of the woman I work for."

"Yes, yes," Lottie said impatiently. "The one who was horrified by the shanty you live in."

"Well, I was wrong! He is just the opposite of what I feared. He is nice to me now. Nicer to me than before." Then she lowered her voice. "I think that he has taken a real interest in me," she confessed.

"You see?" Lottie said. "He knows we are just beginners here. And he doesn't hold it against us."

"Oh, and there's more. He told me he's studying at the university to become a lawyer. Just think of it! A lawyer!"

Lottie tossed her head and said with a modest grin, "I have good news too. Oscar, the glassblower's son, is sweet on me. His family is not rich like the Wallaces, but his father has landed a good job."

"That's wonderful too," Amelia said, smiling at her friend. But she almost pitied her. The girls were the same age, and poor Lottie had a silly, turkey-necked 16-year-old taking a fancy to her. Amelia had attracted a university man.

The two girls parted company, and Amelia bounded off for home. As she hurried through the early evening dusk, her mind raced ahead to the future. Maybe Herman would become a great lawyer and then a politician or a judge. She pictured herself as the wife of such an important man. Then she laughed at her own fantasies. It was probably ridiculous to dream such dreams. But in America one could be a beggar one day and a rich person the next. Amazing things happened here.

As Amelia neared home, she heard Eva Eulmann's racking cough. The sight of the sad young husband's haunted eyes remained with Amelia as she hurriedly went inside the Kintzes' shanty. She closed the door tightly. She was glad she could no longer hear the poor woman coughing out her life.

But quickly, happier thoughts filled Amelia's mind and heart. She remembered Herman's sunny face and smiled. She could hardly wait to go to work the next day.

4

The following Sunday the Kintz family sat down to chicken and dumplings, with apple pie for dessert. Mr. Kintz talked of the addition to the house that would soon be underway. His plans included another large room for sleeping and a loft where Pauline and Tillie would sleep. Amelia would have a small space of her very own. She would have a real bed, a store-bought bed.

Mrs. Kintz's eyes danced with excitement when her husband talked about putting in the wooden floor. "We can decorate it with throw rugs," Mrs. Kintz said. "It will be almost as nice as our home in Bavaria."

Amelia thought that was going too far. Still, it would be much better than what they had now.

After dinner Amelia and Tillie went outside and sat down on a nearby tree stump.

"Herman Wallace tells me I'm pretty," Amelia confided. "I know I'm not really. But it's nice to hear it just the same."

Tillie shrugged her shoulders. Her fat blond braids danced on her back.

"Abigail Wallace is in school with me,"

Tillie said. "Everybody just hates her because she is always bragging. She has a Fanny Gray, one of those new paper dolls that comes in a box with fancy verses. I've never seen anything like it. We all wish we had one. But no one else can spare the money. Still, Abigail doesn't have to boast all the time about what she has."

Amelia was irked by Tillie's words. "You don't know anything about people, Tillie," she said. "You are only 13 years old. I know Herman is a wonderful person. And I cannot imagine that his sister isn't nice too."

Tillie snickered and said, "Herman doesn't really like you, Amelia. He is just making sport of you. You heard what Father said about the way Mr. Wallace spoke of Germans. Herman wouldn't truly like a German girl."

Amelia's irritation turned to anger. "Herman's mother is German. She speaks German as well as we do!"

Tillie shook her head at Amelia. "You are worse than Pauline. Pauline imagines one of the Schmidts' mules will turn into a flying horse and carry her off to a magic island. You imagine that a university boy is taken with you."

"You are a horrible little wretch!" Amelia shouted.

"I don't even think Herman is nice-looking," Tillie taunted. "I saw him once in the dry goods store. He wore dirty gaiters that looked like he had waded in mud. Besides, his teeth are so big. He looks like a mule." Tillie tried to imitate a mule braying. "Eeee-ahh, eeee-ahhh."

Amelia looked around for something to throw at her sister. All she could find was a matted clump of cold, rotting leaves. She picked it up and heaved it at Tillie. Tillie scrambled for revenge. She groped in the dirt for something to throw back. But Amelia quickly ran across the field that separated the Kintzes' shanty from the Millers'.

Tillie gave up the pursuit of her older sister when Amelia reached the Miller house. She knew the fight would be two against one because Lottie and Amelia always stuck together.

Suddenly Tillie tipped back her head, cupped her hands around her mouth, and yelled as loudly as she could, "Herman Wallace doesn't like you. He likes Teresa Blanchard!"

Amelia could hardly believe her ears. Her cheeks reddened with rage and embarrassment. How would Tillie know such a thing? The wicked little monster—how could she possibly know? Unless Abigail Wallace had told her . . . But no, it was a lie. Tillie was just jealous that Amelia had a job and a boy who was interested in her.

Suddenly Amelia heard her mother calling, "Amelia! Come home!"

Amelia ran across the field, ignoring Tillie, who was braying like a mule again. Amelia would not give her younger sister the satisfaction of knowing she had embarrassed her.

Mrs. Kintz was waiting impatiently with two large covered dishes. She handed one to Amelia. "Come along, 'Melia. We're taking these over to the Eulmann house. Poor Moritz has enough to cope with—his sick wife, their young children. It is too much to think about making supper too."

The women in the shanty settlement

often took meals to the Eulmanns because the young father was carrying such a heavy load. Tonight it was the Kintzes' turn. Amelia silently took the dish filled with chicken and dumplings. She walked beside her mother toward the Eulmann house. Her thoughts were not on the food she carried or on Moritz Eulmann's burdens until her mother spoke.

"Our families were very close in the old country," Mrs. Kintz said. "Moritz's parents were saints. When I was a girl about your age, typhoid fever broke out. The Eulmanns helped us. They had seven children of their own, and some of them were sick too. But still they helped us.

"Moritz was not yet five years old, and he would carry buckets of cow's blood for the sickest ones to drink," she continued. "That's what they did—drank the blood of cows. It was what kept some of them alive. My brother was like a skeleton. We would have lost him if not for the Eulmanns."

Amelia shuddered at the thought of drinking cow's blood. But she was still too worried about what Tillie had said to think much of past tragedies. Perhaps Tillie just made up the name of Teresa Blanchard from something she found in a newspaper...

"My poor brother," Mrs. Kintz sighed. "He was so weak, he couldn't walk. The Eulmanns told us to put him in cool water to reduce the fever that was killing him. Then they brought the cow's blood. They saved his life—and many others too. That's why we must help Moritz now. Because of what Moritz's parents did for all of us back in the old country."

Ameila nodded and looked up at the sky. Dismal gray clouds hung overhead, and the air was turning colder. Snow will soon be falling, she thought.

They reached the Eulmann house. It was nicer than most of the other shanties. Moritz was a gifted woodworker. He was able to build a three-room house with a wooden floor as soon as he and Eva had arrived from the old country. At first, everything had looked so promising. They thought that Eva's nagging cough was just a cold she had picked up on the ocean voyage.

But then her cough grew worse, much worse. The doctor said it was more than just a bad cold. It was consumption. And there was very little to be done for it. Sometimes fresh air and healthy food helped, but that was all. That, and to hope for the best.

Moritz Eulmann came to the door now. His serious face was filled with gratitude when he saw Amelia and her mother. "Thank you so much, Margaret. Amelia." He breathed in deeply. "Oh, that smells good. The children will enjoy it."

"You eat some too, Moritz. You are too thin. Look at you. You must keep up your strength," Mrs. Kintz scolded the young man as if he were one of her children.

"I have very little appetite," Moritz said solemnly.

"You eat some chicken and dumplings, Moritz," the older woman continued. "It will do the children no good if you get sick." Then she set the apple pie they'd brought on the table too.

"Oh, how wonderful," Moritz said, looking at Amelia and her mother. "Thank you both for walking over here on such a cold evening to bring all this good food."

Amelia smiled. She was amazed how polite and gracious the young father was in spite of the despair in his eyes. Her heart ached for him and his terrible predicament. "Is there anything else we can do?" she asked.

"No, no," Mr. Eulmann replied, shaking his head. "This is already too much." Little Minnie and Albert crowded around the table. Their eyes were wide with anticipation as they gazed at the covered dishes. The chicken and dumplings was still warm, and its fragrance filled the air.

"How is Eva?" Mrs. Kintz asked.

"She is sleeping now, thank goodness," Moritz replied.

"Who is caring for the children when you work?" Amelia's mother asked.

"I bring work home when I can," Mr. Eulmann answered. "And Eva's sister, Hilda, has offered to come and help out for a short time. As soon as she can get away. She's a piano teacher in Cincinnati."

"Well, if you need anything, please let us know," Mrs. Kintz urged.

"Thank you, Margaret. Thank you," Moritz replied. "That is so kind."

As Amelia and her mother turned to leave, they heard a weak voice from the bedroom. "Thank you, Margaret. Thank you, Amelia. God bless you both." It was Eva. She had not been sleeping after all.

"Rest well, Eva," Mrs. Kintz called.

While they walked down the road, Amelia said, "Poor Eva. Poor children. Minnie's dress looked so ragged. Mrs. Eulmann used to make pretty dresses for her." Then with fresh enthusiasm, she said, "I think I will sew a dress for Minnie! I can get a discount on the fabric at the dry goods store. I will start tomorrow."

"That would be very nice, 'Melia." Mrs. Kintz said.

"Mrs. Wallace hinted that she might give me a raise soon because I am a hard worker," Amelia said. "I think Herman likes me and is telling his mother to be nice to me." She smiled. When she thought of Herman, she felt light-hearted and joyous again. And contrary to what Tillie had said, he did not have mule teeth. He just had a nice full set of white teeth.

Mrs. Kintz glanced at her daughter quickly and shook her head. "Amelia, don't lose your senses because a boy winks at you. Don't follow him blindly down the wrong path," she cautioned.

"Mother, I would never lose my senses over *any* boy," Amelia assured her.

"See that you don't," her mother said.

* * *

The next days were busy. Amelia worked hard for Mrs. Wallace, and she spent her free time sewing Minnie's dress. When she finished, she proudly showed the little blue dress to Herman.

"Very nice, Amelia," he said indifferently. Then he frowned. "You know, I will be returning to the university before very long."

Amelia's heart sank. "When must you go?" she asked. She dreaded the answer.

"Soon. So I hope we do not waste our precious time together," Herman said. He reached into his pocket and pulled out a small book. "Do you like poetry?" he asked.

"Yes, but I cannot read English very

well yet. I practice by reading the newspaper and magazines. But poetry is very hard for me unless it is in German," Amelia answered.

"Let me read a very beautiful poem to you. It was written by a man named Robert Herrick. Do you know his works?" Herman asked.

Amelia was embarrassed again. She had gone to school in Germany until she was 14. Then she stayed home to learn cooking and sewing from her mother. She knew very little about history or poetry or such things that well-educated people knew. "No. I don't think I've heard of him," she admitted.

Herman reached out and caressed Amelia's cheek. "Poor thing," he said. "You are ignorant of so many things. But it is not your fault. Nobody has shown you the finer things in life."

Amelia felt hurt that he had called her ignorant. But she promptly forgave him. After all, he had not called her stupid. One cannot change anything if one is stupid. But there was hope for Amelia. She knew that with effort she could overcome her ignorance. So she listened carefully to Herman, intent upon learning.

"The name of this poem is 'To The Virgins, to Make Much of Time,' " Herman said with a sideways glance at her. He read her the first verse.

Gather ye rosebuds while ye may,
Old time is still a-flying;
And this same flower that smiles today
Tomorrow will be dying.

"Do you know what Herrick is saying, Amelia?" Herman asked.

"I think so," Amelia lied. "But you explain it to me."

"This wise poet is telling young maidens—like yourself—to give pleasure to themselves and to others while they are young and lovely. Because when they are old and gray, there is not much pleasure left to give, is there?" Herman said.

Amelia listened attentively to Herman. He was much more learned than she was. He seemed so much wiser. But what was he really saying? Her face took on a puzzled look.

Herman smiled at her confusion and said, "Let's go out into the country this Sunday. I will pick you up in our buggy. We can go to the woods and sit by the lake. I will read poetry to you. We'll have a fine time together."

Amelia's heart raced. Herman was asking her out on a date! "I will ask my parents when I get home," she promised.

"Tell them that your employer and her son want to take you on a picnic," Herman said.

"Oh, your mother is coming too?" Amelia asked. And she thought perhaps his sister Abigail would come as well.

Herman chuckled and caressed Amelia's cheeks again. "Poor Amelia," he said. "You have much to learn. Just tell your parents what I have told you to tell them, and all will be well."

5

That evening Amelia took Minnie's new blue dress to the Eulmann house. It was not yet spring, but the air was growing warmer. Amelia no longer shivered when she was outside as she had done all winter.

In just a few weeks the Kintz family would put in their vegetable garden. And her father would build the new room. Amelia again looked forward to spring when things might be better.

Amelia carried Minnie's dress, along with a mince pie her mother had made. She rapped lightly on the door. Soon Mr. Eulmann appeared. "Amelia!" he said, smiling. "Please come in."

"I have brought you a mince pie Mother baked and a new dress for Minnie," she said. "I sewed the dress myself," she added proudly.

"How kind you are!" Mr. Eulmann said. "Tell your mother I can never repay her kindness." He took the bundle from Amelia and led her inside.

"How is your wife?" Amelia asked softly.

The man sighed and shrugged his

shoulders. "She is resting. The children are asleep too."

Mr. Eulmann unwrapped the bundle and held up the little blue dress with the fancy collar.

"I do hope it fits her. I made it a bit large so she can grow into it," Amelia said.

"How beautiful it is!" Mr. Eulmann exclaimed. "Amelia, how did you know?"

"Know what?" she asked in surprise.

"Minnie's birthday is on Saturday. She will be four years old," Mr. Eulmann said. "I have been so busy, I have not gotten her anything. Now she has a wonderful dress for her birthday. I am so grateful."

Then he sighed. "I worry about the children. There is so little joy in their lives now . . ." His voice trailed off.

Again, Amelia's heart went out to the haggard-looking young man. It was hard to believe he was just eight years older than she was. "They have you for a father," she said. "Any child would be grateful for that."

"Thank you, Amelia," Mr. Eulmann said. "You always seem to know the right thing to do—and say."

As Amelia made her way home, she thought about Herman's invitation. She had not yet asked her parents if she could go on the picnic with him on Sunday. Something about Herman's advice troubled her. *Just tell your parents what I have told you to tell them, and all will be well.* What did he mean by that? Amelia wondered. Then she shook her head. Herman is a respectful young man, she told herself. And with that, she dismissed her troubled thoughts.

"Mother," Amelia said when she arrived home, "Herman has asked me to go on a picnic Sunday afternoon."

Mrs. Kintz frowned. "What is this? The young man is courting you? You are too young, *liebkin*."

"Oh, no, Mother," Amelia said quickly. "Herman said his mother is asking me because she is happy with my work at the store. It will be . . . a family picnic."

"Oh, well that is a different thing," her mother replied with relief. "You are very young and innocent, 'Melia. But if this is a family outing, then it will be fine. I will make pies for you to bring along."

Amelia felt guilty. She had not exactly lied. But she had spoken deliberately so her mother would get the wrong idea. It was clear to Amelia that Herman's family would not be at the picnic. But it was also clear that her mother would never let her go with Herman alone. And Amelia wanted to go. She wanted to go very much. Herman is such a handsome, charming young man, she thought. He knows so much more than I will ever know. She was thrilled that such a boy found her interesting and attractive.

The next day Amelia confessed to Lottie about the deception. "My parents think I am going on a family picnic with Herman and his family. But it will be just him and me," she confided.

Lottie pursed her lips and squinted her eyes thoughtfully as she studied Amelia. Then she asked, "Do you trust Herman?"

"Oh, yes! With my life!" Amelia insisted. "He is the dearest, most wonderful young man I have ever known. I have felt so sad and lonely here in America. But now, for the first time, I am glad we came. I am so excited and happy. And it's because of Herman."

"Well then, it looks like you did the right thing," Lottie said with confidence.

Amelia grabbed her friend and hugged her. "Oh, Lottie, I knew you would understand. You are my best friend. I don't know what I would do without you!"

The girls sat down on the warming earth and watched the clouds float by. Then Lottie asked, "What will you do if he wants to kiss you?"

"Oh, he won't. He is a perfect gentleman," Amelia answered.

"Oscar tried to kiss me," Lottie confided. "He sneaked up behind me and kissed the back of my head!" She giggled. "He thrust his silly face into my hair, and I spun around. He jumped back like he'd been stung by a wasp. Poor boy! My long yellow hair was stuck to his lips. It was the funniest thing I'd ever seen!"

Amelia laughed. Oscar was a silly boy, but Herman was a fine young man. There was a world of difference.

With her head held high, Amelia walked toward home. I feel beautiful, even in my ragged, faded dress, she told herself. Then she looked down at herself. What would she wear on Sunday? Certainly not the dress she had on. That wouldn't do at all. Nor would any of her other miserable dresses. She would not embarrass Herman by riding in his fine buggy like that. She must be suitably dressed.

There were ready-made dresses for sale in the dry goods store. Ready-to-wear dresses were being produced in all the large cities, and Mrs. Wallace had a nice selection of them. Amelia made up her mind to buy one.

When Amelia went to work the next day, she looked at all the fine dresses in the store. She fingered the fabric on a bright yellow one with a blue sash. Around the scoop neckline was delicate embroidery. The dress was the same color as the crocuses Herman had shown her. She remembered his words, *You should have a dress that color, Amelia. It would make your pretty face even prettier.* This was definitely the dress she wanted.

"Mrs. Wallace, this dress looks just right for me. May I try it on?" Amelia asked.

"Yes, but it is quite dear," Mrs. Wallace said with a frown.

"Yes, I know. But I am making money now. And I can buy one nice dress," Amelia explained. She was reluctant to tell Mrs. Wallace about her date with Herman. Perhaps, like Amelia's own mother, she knew nothing about it.

Amelia carefully slipped into the costly dress and admired what she saw in the mirror. The yellow color was perfect for her dark, curly hair. And Herman was right. It *did* make her look prettier.

"I will have it," she declared, her cheeks flushed with excitement. She could pay for the dress over a period of a month.

Amelia made her way home that evening with the precious dress in a bundle under her arm. She was so excited about Sunday that she didn't think she could bear to wait three more days. Near her shanty, she saw Mr. Eulmann and his children outside. Little Minnie wore her new blue dress. She looked lovely in it.

"Good evening, Amelia," Mr. Eulmann said. "See how proud my Minnie is? Minnie, thank this dear girl for your dress."

Minnie peered shyly from behind her

father's long legs and whispered in German, "*Danke schōn.*"

"*Bitte,*" Amelia said warmly. "You look so pretty, Minnie."

Mr. Eulmann's mood seemed more light-hearted this evening. Perhaps his wife was better, she thought. The doctor said that good food, rest, and fresh air can sometimes work a cure.

"Is your wife any better today, Mr. Eulmann?" Amelia asked.

"She does seem stronger," Moritz replied. "We are thankful for that. We hope it is a good sign. She got out of bed and sat outside in the sunshine for a while today."

"I'm so glad," Amelia responded sincerely.

With the look of desperation momentarily gone from his face, Moritz Eulmann looked handsome once again. His wavy black hair tumbled down over his brow. And his dark eyes sparkled. When his eyes were not sunken in despair, Amelia decided, they were his best feature. Hope had transformed his whole appearance.

When Amelia got home, she looked for her mother. She wanted to tell her of the beautiful dress she had bought. She was sure her mother wouldn't mind since Amelia was working now. But today she found her mother in a dark mood. Usually Mrs. Kintz put up with all the dirt and misery of the shanty. The lice in the collars of the shirts. The dust everywhere. But today she had received a letter from her mother in Germany. In the letter Amelia's grandmother had made it clear that coming to America was not a good decision on her daughter's part.

"Remember where you come from," the letter said. The elderly woman was afraid that Margaret would be corrupted and forced into a miserable life. Her letter continued, "Don't forget, Margaret, that even though you are in America, your home and the appearance of your family still reflect upon our good name."

Now Amelia's mother felt overwhelmed. "This place," she moaned, shaking her head. "This dirty place! A pig would not endure it! We share our house with vermin. How can I keep anything clean with dirt coming in all the cracks of the walls? My mother suspects that we are living like animals. If she knew the true living conditions, she would come across the ocean and get me!"

A wave of pity swept over Amelia. Their little house in Bavaria had been so well-built and so clean that one could eat off the floors. No grimy dirt or vermin ever came near it. But war and revolution swirled around them in Bavaria, leaving little to look forward to. The young German men faced endless military service. The women had to say good-bye to their soldier sons and husbands. And those who were unmarried faced a shortage of young men to court and marry them.

Amelia tried to comfort her mother. "Father is going to make our house better in the springtime. You will see," she said.

"That's what he says. But promises are easier made than kept. I will probably be living in this filthy place until the day I am put in my coffin and buried, God help me!" Mrs. Kintz wailed. Suddenly she looked much too old and tired for a woman not yet 40.

"Mother, in the spring we will have a floor and another room. Then dirt cannot come in the walls. Father will make the walls fast," Amelia said confidently.

Mrs. Kintz sighed and sat down heavily. Her cheeks flushed with anger and exhaustion. Amelia knew this was no time to tell her mother of the dress she had bought. And she could think of no way to comfort her. So Amelia quietly left the room to let her mother brood alone.

6

Mr. Kintz was late in coming home that night. Usually he arrived home from the shoemaker's by 6:00. But tonight it was almost 8:00, and still he had not returned.

Amelia peered outside into the darkness, waiting and wondering. Soon she made out the form of a man walking unsteadily toward their shanty. It was her father! He was singing a lusty song from the old country and swaying his arms to its rhythm.

"Du, du liegst Mir im Herzen," he sang in German.

When Mrs. Kintz heard the singing, her eyes blazed in anger. "He is drunk!" she cried.

Mr. Kintz barged in the front door. His cheeks were flushed, his cap was perched askew on his head, and his mustache was twitching with excitement.

"Margaret!" Mr. Kintz shouted as if she were far away instead of right in front of him. He smelled of beer. As if he had jumped into a beer barrel and remained there for quite some time. Tillie and Amelia watched. They didn't know whether to feel amused or frightened by the sight.

"Jacob!" Mrs. Kintz screamed. She threw her arms in the air in exasperation. "You are drunk! *Dumkopf!* You are drunk!"

Her husband's smile faded. This was obviously not the reception he had expected. "But Margaret . . ." he began.

"Shush!" his wife interrupted. "All day long I have been fighting a losing battle against this filthy place until I am so weary, I am about to perish. And now you come home staggering drunk! You should be ashamed!"

"Margaret, please. Let me explain," Mr. Kintz pleaded.

"What is there to explain?" Mrs. Kintz demanded. "Where do you get the money to spend on beer? We are barely making do, and you are squandering what little we have on drink! Shame! Shame!"

"Margaret, listen, please," Mr. Kintz implored. "Some of my friends celebrated my good fortune with me. Mr. Rieb has given me yet another raise! I am now making eight dollars a week. Eight dollars!"

"Eight dollars!" Mrs. Kintz repeated the

amount in disbelief.

"*Ja.* And he said it might be even more before the summer," her husband said. "Old Rieb has finally admitted that since I began work, his shop's income has increased considerably. Now he is fearful of losing me to a rival cobbler."

"Eight dollars?" Mrs. Kintz asked again as if she were in a trance.

"*Ja, ja,*" Mr. Kintz said, his smile returning to his ruddy face. "Now we can put in the floor and add the new room sooner. And maybe get some nice furniture too."

Suddenly, he took his wife into his arms and began a little waltz across the floor. "*Du, du liegst Mir im Herzen,*" he sang. "You, you are in my heart."

"Stop it, you foolish man," Mrs. Kintz protested. But now she was smiling too. The despair she had felt earlier had turned to hope.

Mr. Kintz warbled on with fresh enthusiasm. And in a few minutes, his wife joined in. They danced together on the dirt floor like that while Tillie and Amelia laughed and clapped happily.

* * *

Sunday afternoon finally came, and Amelia waited in her pretty yellow dress for Herman to arrive.

"You look so pretty, 'Melia," her mother said as she wrapped two mince pies for the picnic. "I am glad you bought such a pretty dress. You deserve something for the hard work you do." She frowned slightly. "I hope this will be enough. How many members of the Wallace family are coming?"

"Two pies will be plenty," Amelia said, avoiding a direct answer to her mother's question.

A few minutes later, Herman arrived in a buggy pulled by a sleek bay horse. When Mrs. Kintz handed him the two pies, she said, "I hope this will feed everybody at your picnic."

"Oh yes, thank you," Herman said with a charming smile. He glanced knowingly at Amelia as if they shared this little deception, this trick they were playing on her mother. Amelia was bothered by Herman's attitude, and yet she remained silent.

As the buggy rumbled away from the settlement, Herman laughed merrily. "How many people did you tell your mother were coming today?"

"Don't laugh about it, Herman," Amelia told him sternly. "It makes me feel terrible."

"How awful if there truly were a whole tribe of my relatives at the lake when we got there!" Herman chuckled as the horse trotted along smartly. "That would spoil everything, eh, Amelia?" He winked at her deviously.

The sun shone brightly that day. Even though the date announcing springtime had not officially arrived, it felt and looked like spring. A few wildflowers peeked out along the roadside. Buds were breaking on the stark trees. In another month everything would be beautiful. Amelia breathed in the fresh air and began to relax.

"My father is now making eight dollars a week at the cobbler's," she said after a while. "We will be building a much nicer house. We will have three rooms instead of one. And we will have a wooden floor too."

"That's good," Herman said. But he didn't seem very interested. Amelia knew that he already lived in a two-story house with seven or eight rooms, a garret, and a cellar. The Wallace home had a nice entry from the street. And although she had never been inside, she envisioned a lovely parlor, a drawing room upstairs, a laundry, and a bright, friendly kitchen. It seemed like a mansion to Amelia.

Amelia remained quiet for the rest of the ride. The woods surrounding the lake still looked barren. But a sprinkling of wildflowers gave color to the otherwise dull landscape. The ice had finally surrendered to the warmth of the sun. And now the dark water shimmered in its bright light.

Herman stopped the carriage and said, "This looks like a nice spot. Do you agree?"

"Yes, it's very nice," Amelia said.

In a gentlemanly manner, Herman helped her down from the carriage. Then they walked a short distance to the edge of the water. There Herman spread the blanket on the ground. Amelia wondered when he would say something about the pretty yellow dress she had selected so carefully. She gathered it around her so it wouldn't get muddy from her shoes. Then she sat down on the blanket.

As she looked out on the lake, Amelia sighed. "It's so beautiful here. It reminds me of the old country, where we lived in Bavaria. Our small village was near a lake."

"Mmm," Herman said absently, sitting down beside Amelia. He didn't seem interested in talking about Bavaria. He removed the poetry book from his pocket. "Shall I continue reading the poem by Robert Herrick?" he asked.

"Please do," said Amelia.

Herman began.

The glorious lamp of heaven, the sun,
The higher he's a-getting,
The sooner will his race be run,
And nearer he's to setting.

Amelia shook her head. "The words are beautiful," she said. "But I'm afraid I don't understand their meaning."

"Herrick is telling young maidens that time is passing very quickly and they will soon be old," Herman explained.

"Oh, I see," Amelia said, nodding her head. "That is true. My mother says that we're old before we know it. Please read on."

Herman smiled and continued.

*That age is best which is the first,
When youth and blood are warmer;
But being spent, the worse, and worst
Times still succeed the former.*

"I think I understand this part," Amelia said. "The poet is saying that youth is the best time of our lives."

"Exactly," Herman smiled. "You catch on quickly, Amelia. Do you agree with what Herrick is saying here? That now is the best time of your life?"

"Oh, yes," Amelia answered. "Youth is wonderful. And I'm certainly not looking forward to getting old."

Herman smiled again. "Shall I finish?" he asked. Amelia nodded eagerly. She was enjoying this discussion of poetry with such a learned young man.

Then be not coy, but use your time,
And, while ye may, go marry;
For, having lost but once your prime,
You may forever tarry.

Amelia looked at Herman questioningly.

"Herrick is telling young maidens—like *you*—" Herman said, "not to waste time being coy around young men. He advises them to be happy *now* with the men they like. For once they've lost their beauty and youth, they will be old and spent for a long time."

"Coy?" Amelia asked. This was an English word she had not heard before.

"Hard to get," Herman answered. "Herrick is saying that young maidens should not worry so much about being modest around young men they are attracted to. Instead they should let their feelings be known—and act on those feelings."

Amelia smiled but wasn't sure what to say. This final message of the poem went against everything she had been taught.

Young girls were supposed to be modest and reserved around boys, not forward. She didn't agree with Herrick—and she knew her parents would never agree either.

Suddenly Herman moved closer to Amelia and placed his arm around her shoulders. His face was so close to her ear that she could feel his breath. "You've never had a boyfriend, have you?" he whispered.

"Yes . . . of course," she answered nervously. She leaned slightly away from him. "I have had boys who liked me but not anything serious."

"Sweet little Amelia," Herman said in a tone of voice one used with helpless animals. "Poor, naive little Amelia. The world is such a mystery to you, eh?" He tightened his grasp around her shoulders.

Amelia was bewildered. She didn't quite know what to say or do. She blurted out impulsively, "I . . . I heard you have a girlfriend named Teresa Blanchard. Is that so?"

Herman pulled his arm back quickly. For a moment he looked upset, even angry. But he promptly regained his composure, and the charming smile returned.

"Where did you hear that?" he asked.

"Your sister told my sister at school," Amelia answered.

Herman laughed lightly and replied, "My sister is always telling tales like that. She is such a little dickens. She spins tales out of nothing. Teresa Blanchard is the daughter of one of my teachers at the university. She is not pretty at all. In fact, she is frumpy and has bad smelling hair because she doesn't wash it. Do you think I would like someone like that?"

Amelia thought it was very unkind of Herman to say things like that about any girl. But she said nothing.

"She is not pretty like you Amelia," Herman continued smoothly. He brushed her dark hair off the nape of her neck. "You are the prettiest girl I've ever seen."

"Thank you," Amelia said, "but—"

"No," Herman said. He put his finger to Amelia's lips. "Don't say anything. Just be with me. Words spoil moments like this."

A cloud passed over the sun, and an

unexpected gloominess settled around them. The air felt chilly. Amelia began to experience an uneasiness inside. She started to get up from the blanket. "Let's take a little walk, Herman," she said as casually as she could manage. She hoped if she moved away from this spot, her growing fears would subside.

But Herman grasped Amelia's hand and pulled her back down beside him. "I'm not in the mood for a walk. I just want to sit here with you," he insisted.

"Herman—" Amelia started. She wanted to tell him she felt uncomfortable.

"I would like to kiss you, Amelia," he interrupted.

"Herman, I like you very much," Amelia said, pulling her arm away from him. "But we don't know each other very well yet, and I don't think we should..."

Herman's smile disappeared from his face as quickly as the sun's brightness under the clouds. "You lied to your parents so you could be alone with me. What did you think would happen?" he chided.

Amelia felt miserable and foolish. "I

thought we would talk and learn more about each other," she said weakly. Her throat was tightening. And she felt tears stinging her eyelids.

"I read you a poem—by a very wise man," Herman snapped. "You smiled at me. You nodded. You said you agreed with him."

Amelia looked down at her pretty yellow dress and bit her lip. She was trying hard not to cry.

"Besides, why would I want to come out here with you to talk?" Herman continued. "What do you have to say that I could possibly be interested in? I am in the university, and you are an ignorant young girl. You knew why we came out here. And now you want to make a game of it. You're not being fair!"

Amelia blinked hard. "I . . . I'm sorry," she said. "I should not have come." She shivered as a cold breeze blew. How could she have made such an error in judgment? she wondered.

"I suppose you want to go home now?" Herman asked crossly.

"Yes," Amelia said, her voice coming out like a weak child's whisper.

"You disgust me," Herman hissed. He stuffed the blanket into the basket carelessly and thrust the mince pies toward Amelia. "Here. You'd better take these home with you."

"I don't want them," she said feebly, not meeting his eyes.

"Then let the squirrels have them," he said as he hurled the lovely pies toward the woods.

"Oh!" Amelia cried. She clasped her hands over her mouth. It was a sin to waste good food like that.

Herman stomped toward the buggy with Amelia hurrying after him. He made no effort to help her into her seat. So she clambered up all by herself, tears trickling down her cheeks.

Herman shouted gruffly at the bay, and the buggy bounded away from the lake. Amelia's bewildered thoughts swirled in her head as they rode along in silence. She thought about Bertha, her older cousin in Bavaria. Bertha had dated a young man when she was only 15. Then the young man vanished, leaving Bertha with a baby to raise. Amelia understood such things could happen. The young man did not care about her. He only cared about himself.

Then Amelia's thoughts turned to her cousins in New York. Her father had said they were ruined. Had they fallen into the same trap as she? Amelia wondered.

Amelia realized now that Herman did not care about her either. He thought she was just an ignorant girl who lived in a shanty. But he thought he could enjoy himself until he went back to the university and found a girl who was more worthy of him.

Angry tears poured down Amelia's cheeks, and she shook with sobs at this knowledge.

7

"Oh stop bawling, will you?" Herman snapped. "You'll be back in that dirty place where you live soon enough, and I'll not bother you again."

His words cut Amelia as sharply as any knife. She could not remember a time in her life when she had felt so miserable. It had been horrible to leave Bavaria, to say good-bye to all her friends. She had felt like she might never see the old country again. Never see Grandmother's pale blue eyes twinkle again. Never share secrets with her cousin Katrina. Oh, how the cousins had wept and clung to each other!

But this was worse. This was worse because she had cared for Herman—and she thought he cared for her too. But now she understood. He cared no more for her than for those mince pies he had hurled into the woods.

The moment the settlement came into view, Amelia started to rise from the seat. When Herman slowed the buggy, she leaped down and ran toward home. She heard him whip the horse, sending the bay off at a gallop. Herman seemed every bit as eager as Amelia to put an end to this horrible day.

Amelia did not know how she could bear to see Herman's face again after this humiliation. And her misery and guilt were all the greater because she had lied to her mother. She should have known better than to think a prosperous young man like Herman would really like her for herself.

" 'Melia," Tillie cried, "home so early?" Seeing Amelia's tear-streaked face, she exclaimed, "Look at you! What happened?"

Amelia was glad that no one else was nearby. Her mother was hanging up the wash with Pauline and Joseph. Mr. Kintz was with his friends. They were planning the new building project.

"I wasn't feeling well," Amelia explained lamely. At that moment, she felt she would rather die than confess to her little sister what had truly happened. She promised herself that she would take this secret to her grave. Unless, of course, she decided to tell Lottie. But she doubted she would even do that.

Tillie peered at Amelia with shrewd blue eyes and said, "You two had a fight, didn't you? I bet he admitted that he had another sweetheart, just like Abigail told me."

Amelia stared at her sister and then answered defiantly, "Let him have a sweetheart if he has one. I could not care less! He is too old for me anyway."

She pushed past Tillie and stomped inside the empty shanty to take off the beloved yellow dress. Now she hated the sight of it. She decided she would never wear another yellow dress in her life. She wrapped the dress in a flour sack and hid it in a big trunk.

Quickly she pulled on one of her plain, faded dresses and tied back her hair. After wiping off her face, she went outside to help her mother finish the wash. The main washing was done during the week. But Joseph's napkins needed washing every day, even on Sunday.

"Well, Amelia, how was the picnic with Herman's family? You certainly didn't stay long," Mrs. Kintz said.

"I was feeling poorly, and so I decided to come home," Amelia answered.

Her mother quickly looked up and

clamped her hand on Amelia's brow. "Well, you don't have a fever," she said with some relief.

"No, no, I am well now. Let me help you fold the napkins," Amelia offered. When she had finished, she picked up Joseph and a clean napkin. Then she escaped inside to change him.

She spent the rest of the afternoon and evening reliving the horrid picnic. How could things have gone so wrong? she wondered. Then she thought about the dry goods store. How could she possibly go back there? How unbearable it would be if Herman were there, scowling at her. But she knew she had no choice. Her family needed the money, and she had no other job.

In the morning Amelia gathered her resolve and forced herself to go to work. To her unhappy surprise, Herman was waiting for her outside the store. He looked harsh. "Mother knows nothing of yesterday," he said in a low, crisp tone. "I warn you. Do not say anything to her."

Amelia looked at Herman, astonished that she could have ever found him attractive. "Why on earth would I say anything?" she asked.

"Just see that you don't," he snapped. "I would not put it past you to tell my mother that I tried to take liberties with you. But I warn you, if you do that, I'll turn the tables on you quickly enough. You know very well that you tempted me from the beginning."

"What?" gasped Amelia. "How can you say that?"

A smile touched his lips, but it was a nasty smile. "I know the sort of people you are," he said, "Your lives are ugly and uncivilized. You exist in squalor and live shamefully. Someone like you is all too eager to lure in a fellow like me whose family has money and good standing in the community."

"How dare you?" she cried. "We are good people. The only sin I am guilty of is trusting you!"

Herman turned and stalked off as Amelia walked into the store. She was shaking in anger. How could she continue to work here? she wondered. How could she bear it? she wondered. Yet her family needed every penny they could get to make a better life. Amelia felt as if she were caught between a rock and a hard place.

* * *

In the long days that followed, it seemed to Amelia that Mrs. Wallace was more cross and demanding than ever. All day long she criticized Amelia for little things. Amelia wondered if her own unhappiness was causing her to be less efficient. Or if Herman had said something to his mother about what had happened. She was glad when each day ended so she could escape to the peace of her own home.

Toward the end of the week, Amelia was passing the Eulmann house when she noticed Dr. Matson's buggy parked outside. The two Eulmann children were playing under a tree where blades of grass were struggling to grow. Minnie had a tiny doll with glass eyes and real hair. The hair looked matted and dirty from overuse. Albert was pushing a wheeled wooden duck back and forth.

They look so bewildered, so lonely, Amelia thought. She knew they could not possibly understand why their mother didn't take care of them anymore. Why she didn't cuddle them or laugh with them. They didn't understand why she coughed so much and slept most of the time. And they did not understand why their father seldom smiled any more.

"Minnie, what a pretty dolly you have," Amelia said, joining the children under the tree. Minnie picked up a corner of her dress and used it to hide her face.

"But Dolly's hair is not clean," Amelia continued. "Look, there's a bucket of soapy water your father used to wash up. Come. Let's wash Dolly's hair."

Minnie clutched the doll against her chest, refusing to give it to Amelia. But Amelia smiled warmly and coaxed, "Dolly wants her hair washed. Won't you help her, Minnie?"

"Dolly wants a bath!" Albert joined in the game. He was eager to see the doll dunked in the water.

Minnie finally nodded and gave up her doll. But her little face was full of worry.

She watched closely as Amelia gently washed the doll's hair and then brushed it dry. The doll's curls were soft and fluffy again. And Minnie's face filled with delight when she reclaimed it.

Then the little girl, hungry for a woman's tenderness, crawled into Amelia's lap with her doll. She snuggled up closely and hugged her tightly. As they sat together on the sparse grass, Amelia turned to Albert who was pushing his duck back and forth.

"Quack-quack," Amelia said in a playful voice.

Albert looked at her, puzzled. "Wack-wack," he mimicked.

Amelia laughed, and the little boy giggled too.

"Quack-quack," Amelia repeated.

The boy quickly said, "Wack-wack, wack-wack." He rocked back on his heels in delight at the sound of the words.

Amelia stayed under the tree playing with the children until Mr. Eulmann came out of the house with the doctor. Dr. Matson had obviously been tending Eva. Now he clapped Moritz on the back and shook his head. Then he said good-bye and hurried toward his buggy.

Mr. Eulmann ran his hands through his hair. He rubbed his brow slowly with his fingertips. When he finally looked up, he noticed Amelia under the tree with the children. He stood for a moment and watched them. He saw Minnie and Albert laughing with Amelia and climbing on and off her lap. Clinging to her. He slowly approached the threesome.

"Amelia," Mr. Eulmann said, "how kind of you to tend the children."

"When I saw the doctor's buggy, I thought you would be busy inside," she replied.

"Thank you so much," Mr. Eulmann said. "I have not seen the children so happy in a long time. I'm afraid I neglect them terribly. Their mother cannot care for them. And they scarcely have a father."

"It's not your fault," Amelia assured him.

"Still," he said, "you have given them a few minutes of joy today. Bless you."

"They are dear children," Amelia said sincerely, getting to her feet. "Good-bye,

Minnie. Good-bye, Albert," she said, giving each of them a hug. "And good-bye, Mr. Eulmann."

She didn't have the heart to ask Mr. Eulmann how his wife was. His tragic face already held the grim answer. There was no good news.

* * *

The next day at the dry goods store, Mrs. Wallace was just as cross as before. Three ladies whose dresses Amelia had altered gave her nice compliments, but that only seemed to make Mrs. Wallace angrier. Amelia was troubled as she worked. Her heart already ached over Herman's treatment of her. And now she couldn't understand his mother's behavior.

At the end of the day Amelia walked to the back of the store. Mrs. Wallace sat at a desk, working on her account book. Amelia summoned all her courage and asked, "Mrs. Wallace, am I no longer satisfactory? You seem to find so much fault with me."

Mrs. Wallace frowned and said,

"It is not the quality of your work that troubles me. I am concerned about your brazen behavior with men."

"Brazen?" Amelia repeated, her heart beating faster. "What do you mean?"

"I know the foul conditions you new immigrants live under. Modesty and decorum are the first to go. I can imagine that your virtue slips away easily," Mrs. Wallace said.

Another insult against her family! Amelia would not stand for this, no matter what the risk. "When have you seen such behavior from me, Mrs. Wallace?" she demanded. "When men come in to pick up things for their wives, have I ever been brazen? Was I brazen to Mr. Mueller yesterday? Or Mr. Haffer today?"

"Well, I have not *seen* you exactly . . ." Mrs. Wallace said in a hesitant voice.

"Then tell me how you know I am brazen!" Amelia ordered. She could not believe she was speaking this way to a middle-aged woman. But her indignation was so great that she had forgotten her timid spirit. She had found courage within herself that she never knew she had.

"I have been told . . ." Mrs. Wallace stammered. "I must admit I've witnessed nothing of the sort, but my son—"

"Your son is a liar—and a scoundrel!" Amelia declared. "He wants to make trouble for me, and do you know why? Because when he invited me to the lake, I would not kiss him and do whatever he liked. I thought your son and I were friends. And we would have a nice talk and learn about each other. But he had other plans. And now he invents lies about me because his *plans* didn't work out!"

Mrs. Wallace's eyes grew large and horrified. She seemed at a loss for words. But Amelia did not doubt that she had just lost her job at the dry goods store.

8

Amelia broke her resolution not to discuss the Sunday incident with Lottie. As the girls sat on a log in the early evening, Amelia told Lottie everything.

"Oh, that vile man!" Lottie cried indignantly.

"I have no doubt lost my job at the store. My parents will be so disappointed," Amelia wailed. "I am so foolish. Why didn't I know in the beginning that Herman was a wicked person? What a *dumkopf* I am!"

"No, you're not," Lottie said loyally. "Herman was very cunning." Suddenly she glanced across the creek that divided the settlement and frowned.

"What's wrong?" Amelia asked, following the other girl's eyes.

"Look," Lottie said. "People are gathering at the Eulmann house."

Amelia's heart sank. "Oh, Lottie! Do you think—" She could not say the dreaded words. Instead, she rushed to her feet and ran into her house. Her father was working late at the shoemakers, and her mother was making supper.

"Mother!" Amelia cried. "Something has happened at the Eulmann house!" Mrs. Kintz set her ladle aside and put Tillie in charge of the two younger children. Then she hurried with Amelia over the little wooden bridge and down the dirt path. Lottie and her mother came as well.

There were already a dozen neighbors crowding into the small house. Mrs. Gerhardt emerged from the bedroom with a somber face. She announced to the others, "Eva Eulmann has died. May she rest in peace."

Amelia stood stock-still, her eyes wide and unbelieving. She had known in her mind that Mrs. Eulmann was dying. But she had never really accepted it in her heart. Somehow she thought Mrs. Eulmann would rally and survive. After all, she was so young—only 22 years old.

As the neighbors thronged, there was little sound but the muffled sobbing of Moritz Eulmann as he held his wife's still body.

The women began talking about bringing food to the family and helping to lay out Eva's body. Mrs. Miller said she would wash the curtains. Mrs. Gerhardt would tidy the house for the showing of the body.

As Amelia listened to the solemn discussion, she suddenly thought of Minnie and Albert. Their mother was dead now. What were they thinking? How terrified they must be with their father sobbing and all the commotion going on around them.

Amelia searched the rooms and quickly found Minnie and Albert crouched in a dark corner of the room they slept in. They clung to each other with frightened eyes. Little Albert was crying. Amelia sat down in the rocking chair and gently lifted them both into her lap. Slowly she rocked back and forth, cuddling them as she crooned softly.

From the other room, she heard a sharp voice she didn't recognize.

"I knew Eva's marriage to that man would come to a tragic end," the voice said. "To move my sister, who was always in delicate health, to this wretched settlement. How can a refined woman be expected to live amid such dirt? It is no wonder she has perished in her youth!"

That must be Eva's sister, Amelia thought. Hilda, the piano teacher from Cincinnati. Amelia had heard about Hilda from Mrs. Kintz. At 30 years of age, neither Hilda nor her twin sister, Hester, were married. Together they taught piano at a studio in Cincinnati. Now Amelia sensed that Hilda had little use for men in general. And even less for Moritz.

"Moritz tried his best," Amelia's mother offered in his defense. "This is one of the better houses."

But Hilda grumbled on bitterly. "In Cincinnati, this would be a place for the chickens! Eva had so many golden opportunities. She was as good on the piano as Hester. We could have all lived in Cincinnati in comfort. But she chose to share the lot of a penniless man and live a life of deprivation and poverty. And what of the children? Motherless little things. There is nothing for them now but an orphanage."

Amelia shuddered at the woman's words. She shielded the children's ears and continued to rock them.

Hilda declared loudly and angrily, "That cabinetmaker has brought my sister to an early grave!"

Amelia looked down at the children. Albert's sobs had given way to sleep. And little Minnie was yawning. Amelia put the children into their bed. She gently tucked a quilt over them. Then she stepped into the back room where Mr. Eulmann still sat beside his wife.

It was a poignant sight. As he held Eva's pale hand, Moritz smoothed her blond hair from her brow and caressed her cheek.

Amelia thought back to their arrival in the settlement. At first Eva had been up and about, doing her chores. She never seemed robust, but she was always cheerful. And she had a sweet smile for anyone who passed by. But consumption seized her soon after the house was built. Her body wasted away until she was little more than a skeleton. But now with her hair against the pillow and her eyes closed as if sleeping, she looked peaceful and beautiful once again.

"I put the children to bed," Amelia said quietly.

WAIT UNTIL SPRING

Even at this terrible moment, he was gracious to her. "Thank you, Amelia," he whispered. Then he shook his head. "My poor children," he said, his voice catching in a soft sob.

"They are sleeping peacefully," Amelia reassured him.

Mr. Eulmann shook his head in grief. "I would have given my life to save her. My precious Eva . . . my dear, sweet Eva. But there was nothing . . . the doctor said the milk, the fresh air . . . but nothing helped . . . nothing."

"I'm so sorry," Amelia whispered.

Amelia and several of the women worked late into the night at the Eulmann house. As was customary when someone died, the body was laid out in the house. Everything was made to look as nice as possible because all the neighbors would come to pay their respects. With so many helping hands, the preparations were soon completed.

Three days later, Eva Eulmann's funeral mass was held in St. Peter's Church, which most of the people in the settlement attended. Almost everyone from the settlement came to the funeral. They walked with the heartbroken, young husband to the graveyard behind the church.

Though the settlement was new, the church cemetery already had many markers. Life was difficult, and cholera and consumption were scourges that claimed the lives of many.

Following the funeral, Amelia and some of the women accompanied Mr. Eulmann back to his house. Amelia held Albert on her arm and led Minnie by the hand. Soon after they arrived, Hilda ushered the women outside so she could speak privately with her brother-in-law. She flashed a look at Amelia, willing her to leave too. But Amelia took the children into the other room instead and began reading them a story.

Hilda proceeded to speak her mind to Moritz Eulmann as if Amelia were not there. And although a wall separated the rooms, the two voices from the front room were loud and clear.

"I must be getting back to Cincinnati, Moritz," Hilda said. "To my students. But before I go, we must settle the children's future. There is a fine orphanage in Cincinnati. One for boys and the other for girls. I will gladly take them there when I leave. My sister and I will make the arrangements."

"Hilda! My children have lost their mother. Do you want them to lose their father too?" Mr. Eulmann cried in anguish.

"How can you care for two small children?" Hilda asked. "This is not the time for sentimental hopes. You are in the shop all day, making cabinets. What will become of the children?"

Hilda didn't give him time to answer. Instead she continued in a businesslike voice. "No, they will be much better off in an orphanage. Later on if you marry again, you might be able to make a home for them. But right now there is no other solution."

"I will not have it!" Mr. Eulmann almost sobbed. "I will not give up my little ones!"

"Moritz, you were always such a foolish man! That is what possessed you to bring my poor sister and the children to this ugly, hopeless place. How can you care for the children? Answer me that!" Hilda demanded, her voice growing dramatic and high-pitched. "You must not destroy the children in the same sinkhole of poverty and disease that has stolen my sister away."

"But—" Moritz began.

"In the orphanage," Hilda continued, cutting off her brother-in-law, "the children will be clean and cared for. And they will receive schooling. It is their only hope to rise above their tragic fate!"

Amelia's heart went out to poor Mr. Eulmann. On this day of all days, when he had just buried his beloved wife, this shrewish woman was pressuring him to give up his children too!

Amelia continued reading the story of a bear cub to the children. But her mind was racing. Then something rose in her. Some powerful emotion shook her, and she knew she couldn't sit in that room like a frightened little rabbit any longer. Not for another minute! She was a young woman, someone who had been paid for her labor. She was not without the respect of others. True, Herman had shamed her.

But mature women at the dry goods store asked her advice about colors and fabrics. She had been praised for making perfect alterations on dresses.

So Amelia stepped into the front room now and said in a firm voice, "Mr. Eulmann, I could care for your children while you are at work."

The offer stunned Mr. Eulmann and silenced Hilda for a moment. They both stared at her. Then Hilda recovered her wits and spoke up. "But you are a seamstress, aren't you? What about the wages you earn to help your own family?"

Mr. Eulmann spoke quickly. "I could offer you three dollars a week, Amelia. The cabinet shop is growing, and your wages would increase. I could let your family have some of the milk, cream, and cheese from our cow as well."

Amelia's head was spinning. She earned four dollars a week at the dry goods store. But the milk from the Eulmann cow would more than make up for the lost dollar. Besides, while the children were napping, she could sew for ladies she already knew. And she had probably lost her job at the dry goods store anyway.

"Yes, I will work for that," Amelia agreed. "I will be with the children while you are at work, and then I will have only to cross the bridge to be home. I won't have that long walk from town like I now have. It will do nicely for me."

Hilda looked furious. "This is not sensible!" she argued. "You are but a girl yourself."

"I shall be 17 in the summer," Amelia replied. "And I am good with the children and clever at housework."

Hilda turned to her brother-in-law. "Surely you will not allow some ragged child from a vermin-infested shanty to raise your children, Moritz. Eva's children! Eva would want something better for her poor, motherless children. How shall she rest in peace?"

"Hilda," Mr. Eulmann answered in a weary voice, "my darling wife drew a promise from me before she died: that I would give my love and attention to our children with all my heart and soul. I will do that now. And Amelia Kintz is heaven-sent to help me."

Hilda glared at Amelia. Her dark, bitter look left no doubt that she blamed Amelia for spoiling her plans. Her plans to yank the children away from this man she despised.

"You take on a lot, child," she said. "You set for yourself a daunting task. My sister was a cultured, intelligent woman with musical gifts. You are obviously without learning, without graces. And yet you expect to be the guardian of these poor children? With you they will never be able to rise to a higher level. Instead they will be brought down to the disgusting level of this poisonous place!"

Amelia was hurt by the woman's hateful insults. But she straightened her shoulders and said in a strong, clear voice, "I come from fine, decent people, ma'am. I think Mrs. Eulmann would be pleased that I will love her children in her own home, with their father near. I think Mrs. Eulmann has been carried to God by the angels, and now she smiles at me. That is what I believe."

Amelia turned her back to Hilda

and opened her arms to the frightened children. They buried their little faces in her skirt. And Amelia embraced them, like a mother hen covering her chicks with her wings.

9

"I should have asked you first before I agreed to work for Mr. Eulmann," Amelia told her parents that night. "But it seemed the right decision to me."

Mrs. Kintz brought some *kuchen*, warm and delicious to the table. She smiled as she sliced the dark bread stuffed with raisins and nuts. "You did the right thing," she said to her daughter.

"I am pleased with you, *liebkin*," Mr. Kintz added.

"May I be the one who goes to the Eulmann house to milk the cow?" Tillie asked.

Her mother smiled and said, "That is up to Amelia. She is the lady of that house now."

"Yes, Tillie, you may," Amelia agreed.

"What about Mrs. Wallace at the dry goods store?" Mrs. Kintz asked. "Won't she be angry that you have quit so suddenly?"

"I sent word to her that I was busy helping the Eulmanns. Tomorrow I will go and tell her I have a new job," Amelia said.

"Just think of it!" Tillie cried excitedly. "We will have all the fresh milk we need, and we can have butter and cheese. And even ice cream!"

"I shan't be shaking cream in a pan of salt and ice with all my other chores," Mrs. Kintz said with mock rebuke. "If we become rich enough for one of those freezers that is cranked, then you shall have ice cream."

Tillie and Amelia grinned.

"It is sad to think Eva Eulmann will not see the springtime come," Mr. Kintz reflected. "Our first springtime in America."

"Maybe it shall also be springtime in Heaven," Tillie said hopefully.

Amelia nodded. "It is always springtime in Heaven, Tillie."

"Father, are we going to plant many vegetables in the spring?" Tillie asked.

"*Ja*, many vegetables," her father answered. "Old Rieb said the soil here is even better than in Germany. It is very rich and dark. We will have lettuce and big tomatoes. And beans and potatoes and celery. Oh, and cabbage too." He chuckled. "Lots of cabbage for sauerkraut, *ja*, Margaret?"

"If there is a root cellar," his wife said. "You promised there would be a root cellar to store the produce for winter, Jacob."

Mr. Kintz grinned. "*Ja*, a big root cellar under the room we are building. In the spring everyone will come and help. Gerhardt and Miller and Kirschner. And when they build onto their homes, I will help them too," he said.

"Mr. Eulmann said he would build some cabinets for us," Amelia reported eagerly. Moritz had felt such gratitude when Amelia came to his rescue that he had offered to help in whatever way he could.

"Such big plans, Jacob," her mother said. "I am just afraid they will come to nothing."

"Wait until spring, Margaret. Then you will see. A fine big root cellar, a new room, a solid floor," her husband promised.

On Sunday the Kintz family went to mass. As usual, Father Hoffer delivered the sermon in German since most of the families in the parish were still struggling to learn English. Amelia spotted Mr. Eulmann with his children. Albert sat contentedly on his lap, and Minnie snuggled up next to him.

After the service Mr. Eulmann sent the children with the Millers. He walked down to the graveyard alone.

Only a few days earlier Mrs. Eulmann had been laid to rest. As Amelia watched, she noticed that Mr. Eulmann no longer wept. But his young face was still disfigured with sorrow.

Instead of walking home with her family, Amelia joined Mr. Eulmann in the cemetery. He stood in silence at his wife's marker. His head was bowed low. When he noticed Amelia, he mumbled, "Would that I lay buried with her."

"The children need you," Amelia whispered.

Moritz nodded. "I wish I had flowers to put by her marker. A pretty bouquet of flowers..."

"There will be many flowers in the spring," Amelia said.

"Yes," Moritz said, "Eva loved flowers. More than anything else, she missed the flower garden we had in the old country." His voice was choked and pitiful.

Amelia wanted to comfort him. But all she could offer was reassurance about his children. "I will be at your house early tomorrow to care for Minnie and Albert," she said.

"Yes. Their faces light up when they see you," he replied gratefully. "It would be so much harder to go to the shop and leave them with someone they do not know."

Later in the day Amelia reluctantly paid a visit to the Wallace house. She had to explain why she wouldn't be coming back to the dry goods store. And she wanted to collect the $1.60 still owed her from her last week's wages.

She walked up to the fine oak door and rapped several times. Within moments a pretty young woman appeared.

"I'm here to see Mrs. Wallace," Amelia said politely.

"Won't you come in?" the young woman offered. Amelia wondered who she was. She seemed too well-dressed to be a servant.

Once inside the parlor, Amelia didn't want to stare at all of the beautiful furnishings. But she couldn't help herself.

Ornaments of brass, china, and glass. Elegant fabrics in rich colors—satins, silks, and brocades. Chairs and sofas with gracefully curved backs and arms.

"The furniture was made by Duncan Phyfe," the young woman explained, noticing Amelia's interest. "Surely you've heard of him."

"No, I don't think so," Amelia admitted.

"Well, he was a famous Scotch cabinetmaker whose work is desired all over the world. When my fiancé and I decorate our home in Philadelphia, we will have some chairs by Phyfe," the young woman said.

"I work for Mrs. Wallace at the dry goods store," Amelia explained. "But I've taken another job. And I am here to collect my pay for the time I worked last week."

"I believe Mrs. Wallace is arriving now," said the young woman when she heard the front door open.

Mrs. Wallace stepped into the parlor. Her eyes fell immediately on Amelia. She glared at her. "You! What are you doing here? You left your job without any notice and put me to a great deal of trouble!" she said, glaring at Amelia.

"I'm sorry, Mrs. Wallace," Amelia apologized. "I left word for you. I was needed by the Eulmann family. I . . . I am here for the wages I earned last week. One dollar and sixty cents, I believe."

"Indeed!" Mrs. Wallace said. "You have the gall to ask for your wages? You shall not see a penny of them. Do you hear me? Now off with you!"

"But Mrs. Wallace—" Amelia began.

"Off!" Mrs. Wallace barked imperiously. Then she turned and left the room.

As Amelia turned to go, she glanced at the woman who had answered the door.

"I do hate unpleasant moments like this," the young woman said, her face flushed with embarrassment. "Herman's mother is quite high-strung. But thankfully her son is a perfect gentleman. I suppose all new brides must contend with the foibles of their mothers-in-law."

Amelia stared at her. "You are marrying Herman Wallace?" she asked slowly.

"Why, yes. Oh, I don't believe I've introduced myself. I am Teresa Blanchard.

Herman and I are getting married in just a few weeks," she said proudly.

So this genteel young woman was the frumpy girl with the bad-smelling hair? Amelia wondered what Teresa would say if she knew what Herman had said about her. "I'm sure you and Herman will be very happy," she mumbled.

She reached for the door handle, but Miss Blanchard's voice stopped her. "You poor thing. Shall I give you a few coins? I can see you are in need of money, and . . . I pity you."

"*You* pity me?" Amelia asked. She almost laughed. Teresa Blanchard had no idea which young woman in that room deserved pity.

WAIT UNTIL SPRING

10

The weather turned warm over the next two weeks. Wildflowers sprang up everywhere, giving the drab gray settlement the colors of an artist's palette. Bursts of yellow, pink, white, blue, and lavender blossoms sprouted beside every shanty. They grew wild, asking for no care.

Some of the families had brought seeds from the old country so that they might have gardens like they left in Germany. Gardens with pansies, petunias, snapdragons, and daisies.

Sounds of sawing and hammering filled the air as men and boys built floors, put in windows and porches, and repaired walls. Neighbors worked together at one project. Then they moved on to the next.

Amelia went to the Eulmann house each day during the week and cared for the children. She stayed until Mr. Eulmann returned in the early evening. Amelia admired the way Moritz Eulmann kept his sorrow to himself. He was always pleasant to her. He complimented her for how well she cared for the children and how neatly she kept the house.

Each evening Amelia prepared supper and then set the table so the young father and his children could eat together. Then she walked home to have supper with her own family.

One Friday as Amelia prepared to go home, Mr. Eulmann said, "You are such an important part of the children's lives. They miss you when you are not here."

"I miss them too," Amelia admitted. Then an idea came to her. "Our family is having a picnic on Sunday after church. Mother always packs a large basket. You and the children would be most welcome." She added, "Minnie and Albert could play with Pauline and Joseph."

"How kind of you," Mr. Eulmann answered. "I'm sure the children would enjoy that. But would it be acceptable to your family?"

"Oh, yes," Amelia said. "My parents always welcome your family."

"Then we will come," Mr. Eulmann said. "It will be such fun for the children. Thank you, Amelia. You are truly heaven-sent."

As Amelia walked toward home, she thought about Mr. Eulmann. He was so kind, so admirable, so brave. She thought about his fine profile and his boyish good looks. He was only 24, and she was almost 17. Not so many years between them. After all, Mother had been only 18 when she married Father, and he had been 24 . . .

But quickly Amelia scolded herself. What was she thinking? Poor Eva! Dead for such a short time. It was not right to feel this way! She must not breathe a word of it. She must suppress these unsettling feelings that stirred within her. It was utter nonsense anyway, she told herself. Mr. Eulmann was a serious, sorrowing widower, and she was just a silly girl. She must not even think such irrational thoughts.

Sunday was warm and beautiful as the Kintzes walked down to the river carrying their picnic baskets. The water flowed along swiftly, and the sun's rays danced on the river's ripples.

Her parents looked happier than she had seen them in months, Amelia observed. Mr. Kintz sported a fine new hat. And Mrs. Kintz wore a new lavender dress she and Amelia had made. With the promise of spring and better times ahead, they were almost like newlyweds.

Half an hour after their arrival, Mr. Eulmann and his children joined them. As the tall man approached, Amelia noticed that neither he nor the children were smiling. It occurred to Amelia that when she was with the children, they smiled and played. But when they were with their father, they became as somber as he was.

"Look how sad he is," Amelia's mother said, shaking her head. "Poor man. He is grieving so much for Eva."

"For the sake of the children, he must be more cheerful," Mr. Kintz advised.

When Minnie and Albert saw Amelia, their frowns gave way to smiles. They ran to her, flinging themselves into her arms. A few minutes later, the two children joined Pauline and Joseph. Happily they rolled, tumbled, and chased one another.

Amelia and Tillie sat with their parents and Mr. Eulmann. Together, they watched the little ones play.

"Look how happy they are together," Amelia observed.

Mr. Eulmann nodded. "Bless the children. They do not feel grief in their bones as we who are older do."

"Moritz," Mr. Kintz said, "I know your loss is heartbreaking. But you must not live as if you died also. It is too hard on the children to see you this way."

Mr. Eulmann took a long, deep breath and shuddered. "I feel as if I have died, Jacob," he said. "I wake in the morning and tend the children. I go to the shop and build cabinets. But it is all done without happiness. Eva was my light, my sun. And her death has left me in darkness."

Mrs. Kintz reached over and touched his shoulder. "Time will heal you, Moritz. You cannot dwell on your loss and make your children feel like they live in a tomb."

"I cannot help myself," he said shaking his head slowly. "Every time it seems there is light breaking through, I remember that my wife is gone. Whatever happens in my life, she will not share it with me now. We used to laugh together, walk together." His voice caught in his throat. "I cannot bear it," he whispered.

Seeing the depth of Mr. Eulmann's

misery, Amelia felt as if her own heart would break. But she had no words to comfort him.

"Each morning on my way to work, I go and visit Eva's grave," Moritz continued. "I know she is not there. I know she is with her Maker. But I must go every day and put something there—a flower, a candle..."

"You should not go every day," counseled Mr. Kintz.

"You don't understand," Mr. Eulmann said gravely. "Eva and I were playmates as children. We always knew that someday we would be married. Without her encouragement, I would have become nothing. And now without her, I am nothing."

"You are much more than nothing," Amelia spoke now with a strong voice. "You are a good father and a fine man. You build beautiful cabinets that everyone in the settlement wants to own. Your furniture is more beautiful than Duncan Phyfe's."

Mr. Eulmann looked up, startled. "Duncan Phyfe was the world's greatest cabinetmaker!" he exclaimed.

"But someday your work will also be famous. And people everywhere will seek it," Amelia insisted.

"Amelia, you are too kind," Mr. Eulmann said with a thin smile.

"It's the truth," she replied staunchly. "You are a fine craftsman."

Mrs. Kintz brought out the fried chicken, potato salad, and apple pies. Everybody ate heartily, except Mr. Eulmann, who picked at his food.

When it was time to go home, Mr. Eulmann attempted to gather his children. But Albert would not come at once. He was playing hide-and-seek, dodging behind trees to avoid his father. He was being playful, but Mr. Eulmann did not smile. Instead, he said in a weary voice, "Come along, Albert. I have no heart for this."

Albert came out from behind the tree obediently, with a face as sad as his father's.

As Mr. Eulmann vanished down the path with his children, Amelia's father frowned and said, "He is casting a shadow over the lives of those little ones. It is sad enough that they must live without a mother. But it must be dreadful to live with a father who has forgotten how to smile."

Amelia had heard that people sometimes died of grief. She didn't know if it ever truly happened. Her grandmother had once told her about a little girl in Bavaria who had lost her mother when she was eight. The child died soon after. Perhaps she died of something unrelated. Or perhaps she died of a broken heart. Maybe if a person stops wanting to live, Amelia thought, something happens to stop the heart that's weak with grief.

Amelia couldn't sleep that night for worrying about Mr. Eulmann. If anything happened to him, the poor children would end up in an orphanage after all. She had grown to love the children and couldn't bear the thought of losing them.

When she arrived at the Eulmann house the next morning, Mr. Eulmann was as somber as usual.

"I have some flower seeds," Amelia said cheerfully. "The children and I will start a garden along the side of the house. We

WAIT UNTIL SPRING

will plant petunias and snapdragons now so they will bloom in the summer."

"That will be nice," Mr. Eulmann said without emotion. He turned then and started down the road toward his shop. As he walked, he gathered wildflowers from the side of the road. Soon he had a small bouquet. Amelia knew he would stop at the cemetery behind the church as always. She stood with the children and sadly watched him go.

Day after day as early spring turned to late spring, Mr. Eulmann's melancholy never lifted. Amelia could hardly bear to look at him. He was such a good, kind man with so much to give his children. Someday he would make a very fine husband to some woman. But that could never happen unless he healed.

"Is Papa sick?" Minnie asked one day. "Sick like Mama was?"

Amelia noticed the worry in the little girl's voice. "No, Minnie," she said soothingly. "Your papa is not sick. He just feels very sad."

"I wish Papa would smile sometimes.

Will he ever smile again, 'Melia? Like before?" Minnie asked.

"I hope so," Amelia said as she gathered the little girl into her arms. She ached from the sadness in the child's eyes.

As she stroked Minnie's soft hair, Amelia realized she ached for another reason too. It was clear. She loved Moritz Eulmann. Though none suspected it, she knew it was true . . . and she would die rather than reveal this secret to anyone. But still she loved him. It was not like the explosive feeling she had had for Herman. This feeling had grown very slowly, like a strong tree grows. And each day she loved him a little more.

* * *

Spring turned to summer. The petunias and snapdragons grew strong and bloomed in a bright array of wonderful colors alongside the Eulmann house.

Amelia grew and bloomed too. She was now 17, tall, and prettier than she'd ever been. Everyone noticed the healthy glow of color in her cheeks.

"You must be in love," Lottie teased. But Amelia just smiled and talked of other things.

One warm, sunny morning Amelia and the children gathered a bright bouquet of snapdragons. They followed Mr. Eulmann at a distance as he walked to the cemetery. When he arrived at his wife's grave, he knelt beside the marker. It read,

Eva Eulmann, born 1834, died 1856.
May the Angels take her Home.

Amelia and the children stood back and watched quietly. Then Amelia led the children forward to the grave. When they reached their father's side, Mr. Eulmann looked up in surprise.

Amelia and the children leaned over and gently placed their flowers on the grave.

"Does Mama like the flowers?" Minnie whispered.

"Yes," Amelia answered. "Your mama is smiling on us. She wants us to be happy. Let's blow her a kiss, shall we?"

Amelia lifted each child up in turn to throw a kiss skyward.

"See, Papa," Minnie said, "we are blowing kisses to Mama." Mr. Eulmann watched but said nothing. Tears sparkled in his dark eyes.

The next morning as Amelia arrived at the Eulmanns, she saw an unexpected sight. Mr. Eulmann was running around the side of the house after a little woolly puppy. In a wild attempt to grab it, Mr. Eulmann tumbled into a mud puddle in front of the house.

He rose with the muddy puppy in his hands and his shirt and trousers drenched. And the children broke into wild laughter. They clapped their hands gleefully and ran to hug their new pet. The puppy squirmed to lick their upturned faces.

Just then Mr. Eulmann spotted Amelia. His lips trembled as if he were about to cry. But instead, he smiled. It was a small, quick smile. An embarrassed smile. It was the first joyous smile Amelia had seen on his face in a long time.

"Come. Join our little family, Amelia," Moritz called. Then he did something that surprised Amelia. He walked toward her and held out his hand. Smiling, she took it.

A year later, in the spring of 1858, Amelia Ann Kintz married Moritz Albert Eulmann in St. Peter's Church. Minnie Eulmann wore a beautiful blue dress with a lace collar, and she carried a basket of colorful snapdragons and petunias. Albert giggled in his serious black suit.

In time the Eulmann Cabinet Shop moved to Cleveland. It was renamed "Eulmann & Sons" to include Albert and the four sons born to Amelia and Moritz. The Eulmanns lived in a nice house with two stories, a cellar, and a garret.

And sometimes they returned to the little shanty settlement to visit Amelia's family. The shanties had become tidy frame houses with green lawns and flower gardens. The neighbors always welcomed Amelia and Moritz. And late into the night the German Americans would laugh and dance to the "Beer Barrel Polka" and "*Du Du Liegst Mir Im Herzen.*"

Novels by Anne Schraff

PASSAGES
An Alien Spring
Bridge to the Moon (Sequel to *Maitland's Kid*)
The Darkest Secret
Don't Blame the Children
The Ghost Boy
The Haunting of Hawthorne
Maitland's Kid
Please Don't Ask Me to Love You
The Power of the Rose (Sequel to *The Haunting of Hawthorne*)
The Shadow Man
The Shining Mark (Sequel to *When a Hero Dies*)
To Slay the Dragon (Sequel to *Don't Blame the Children*)
A Song to Sing
Sparrow's Treasure
Summer of Shame (Sequel to *An Alien Spring*)
The Vandal
When a Hero Dies

PASSAGES 2000
The Boy from Planet Nowhere
Gingerbread Heart
The Hyena Laughs at Night
Just Another Name for Lonely (Sequel to *Please Don't Ask Me to Love You*)
Memories Are Forever

PASSAGES to History
Dear Mr. Kilmer
Dream Mountain
Hear That Whistle Blow
Strawberry Autumn
Winter at Wolf Crossing